For Aretha Franklin
—Barb

For my dad, Ron Graef, and all those who worked in the automobile industry
—Renée

Barbara, Renée, and Sleeping Bear Press wish to thank the following organizations and businesses for their assistance. A special thank-you goes to Devin Scillian.

Detroit Metro Convention & Visitors Bureau
Detroit Foundation Hotel
Detroit Riverfront Conservancy
Ford Piquette Avenue Plant
Fox Theatre
Charles H. Wright Museum of African American History
Motown Museum
Detroit Institute of Arts

Renée would like to thank Cathy Holly and Sarah Rhoads.

Text Copyright © 2019 Barbara Joosse • Illustration Copyright © 2019 Renée Graef
Design Copyright © 2019 Sleeping Bear Press • All rights reserved.
No part of this book may be reproduced in any manner without the express written consent
of the publisher, except in the case of brief excerpts in critical reviews and articles.
All inquiries should be addressed to: Sleeping Bear Press™
2395 South Huron Parkway, Suite 200, Ann Arbor, MI 48104
www.sleepingbearpress.com © Sleeping Bear Press
Printed and bound in the United States • 10 9 8 7 6 5 4 3 2 1
Library of Congress Cataloging-in-Publication Data
Names: Joosse, Barbara M., author. | Graef, Renée, illustrator.
Title: Lulu & Rocky in Detriot / written by Barbara Joosse ; illustrated by Renée Graef.
Other titles: Lulu and Rocky in Detroit
Description: Ann Arbor, MI : Sleeping Bear Press, 2019. | Series: Our city adventures ; book 2
Identifiers: LCCN 2019004062 | ISBN 9781534110182 (hardcover)
Subjects: LCSH: Detroit (Mich.)—Guidebooks—Juvenile literature.
Children—Travel—Michigan—Detroit—Guidebooks—Juvenile literature.
Classification: LCC F574.D43 J67 2019 | DDC 977.4/34—dc23
LC record available at https://lccn.loc.gov/2019004062

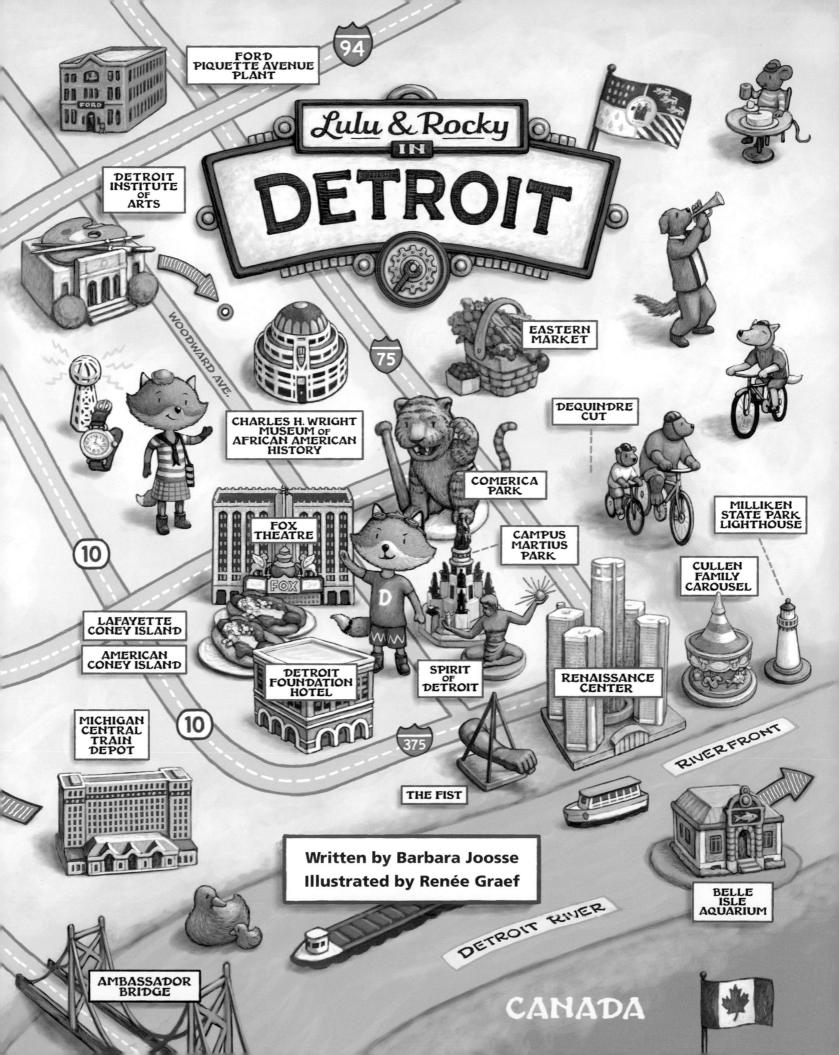

Lulu & Rocky
IN
DETROIT

Written by Barbara Joosse
Illustrated by Renée Graef

FORD PIQUETTE AVENUE PLANT

DETROIT INSTITUTE OF ARTS

WOODWARD AVE.

CHARLES H. WRIGHT MUSEUM OF AFRICAN AMERICAN HISTORY

EASTERN MARKET

DEQUINDRE CUT

COMERICA PARK

MILLIKEN STATE PARK LIGHTHOUSE

FOX THEATRE

CAMPUS MARTIUS PARK

CULLEN FAMILY CAROUSEL

LAFAYETTE CONEY ISLAND

AMERICAN CONEY ISLAND

DETROIT FOUNDATION HOTEL

SPIRIT OF DETROIT

RENAISSANCE CENTER

MICHIGAN CENTRAL TRAIN DEPOT

THE FIST

RIVER FRONT

BELLE ISLE AQUARIUM

AMBASSADOR BRIDGE

DETROIT RIVER

CANADA

A purple envelope arrives.

Dear Rocky,

Are you ready for three days of adventure? Join Lulu and her friend Pufferson and motor to Detroit in a classic Ford coupe. Then head to the Foundation Hotel.

Aunt Fancy

Rocky Fox

Lulu's my cousin AND best friend. She gets her invitation by e-mail.

"MR. CRAZYPANTS!" yells Lulu,
who's as fizzy as a shook-up pop bottle.

We bear-hug and fox-box.
Then we smoosh together in this super-cool
car and I really, really want to go FAST!

But Pufferson is *always* careful. So. He. Drives. Slooooooow.

"Welcome to the Foundation Hotel," says Mr. Reggie, the concierge. Then he winks and says, "You three are as cute as a bug's ear."

The Foundation Hotel is full of little lights that make me feel like I'm in the middle of Christmas. It used to be a fire station, and there are big red doors where the fire engines once passed and also fire poles and a table where you can do puzzles and games.

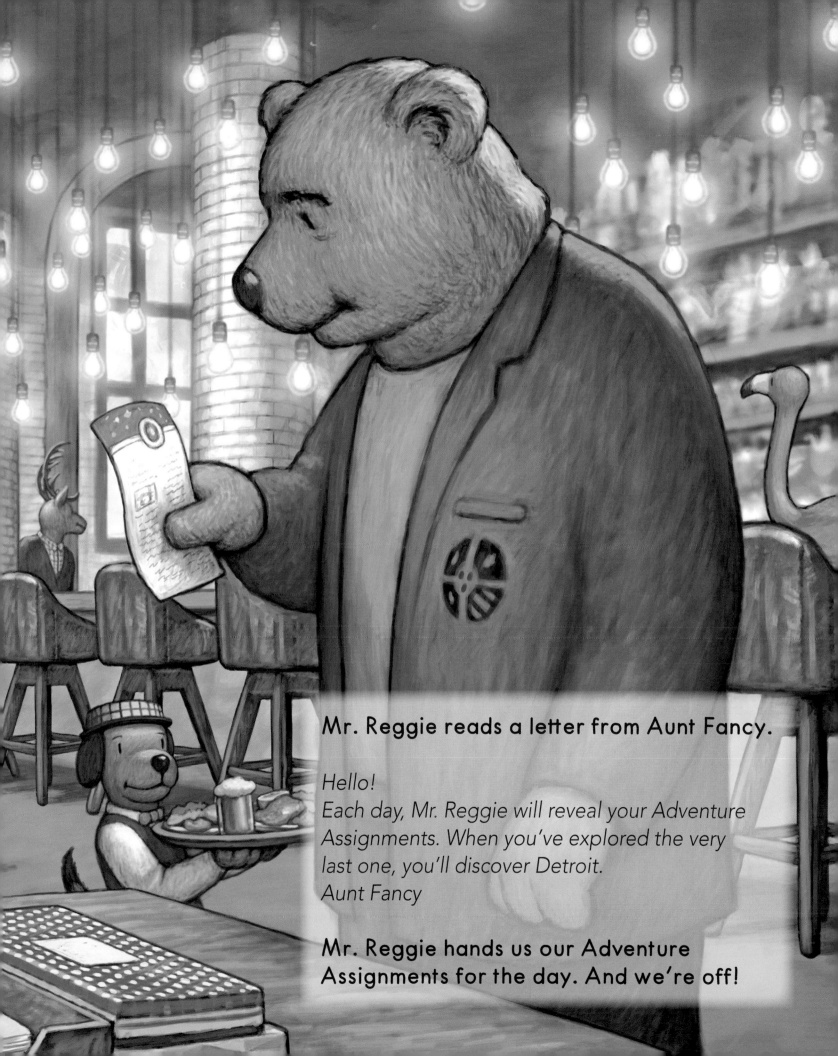

Mr. Reggie reads a letter from Aunt Fancy.

Hello!
Each day, Mr. Reggie will reveal your Adventure
Assignments. When you've explored the very
last one, you'll discover Detroit.
Aunt Fancy

Mr. Reggie hands us our Adventure
Assignments for the day. And we're off!

First, we walk to Campus Martius, an excellent place to make sandcastles. Pufferson makes a sand igloo.

Next up, coney dogs. But which diner's best?
Lulu tries Lafayette. I try American.

"American's top dog!"

"Lafayette!"

"American!"

"Lafayette!"

Then we hop on the People Mover . . .

Lulu whispers,
"I feel like I'm
in a palace."

After the show, we cross the street to sports fan heaven, where the stadiums for four teams—the Red Wings, the Lions, the Pistons, and the Tigers—are close by. At Comerica Park, we hear the best sound ever.

Crack! "That one is *looong* gone!"

Lulu and I ride along the Dequindre Cut. Pufferson's legs are too short to reach the bike pedals, so he rides with me. Later, he sends a picture to Aunt Fancy.

That night, Mr. Reggie asks, "What did you discover?"

"Detroit is fancy, like a palace," says Lulu.

"And sporty, like a stadium," I say.

"Detroit is that, and more," says Mr. Reggie. Then he hands us our Adventure Assignments for tomorrow.

Our first assignment is Eastern Market. We buy cherries.

Oopsie-daisy.

At Belle Isle, we visit the aquarium.
Later, we fish from a pier.

When we catch, we release,
so the aquarium fish aren't sad.

At the Charles H. Wright Museum of African American History, we learn about heroes from Africa to Detroit.

We are inspired.

Hitsville U.S.A. is home of the Motown Sound,
where everybody sings together in harmony,
making their voices sound like one. When we sing
to Aunt Fancy, we pretend we're the Three Tops.

The next day, we explore the Ford Piquette Avenue Plant, where Henry Ford designed and built the first Model T. In the beginning, his inventions weren't perfect. But they kept getting better.

We crank the engine with the flywheel magneto and check out Henry Ford's Secret Experimental Room. Now I want to be an inventor too.

Our next Adventure Assignment is the Detroit Institute of Arts. We walk through the gate to . . .

Lulu says, "This makes me feel small on the outside and big on the inside."

The Riverfront is Detroit's "hello place,"
where everybody greets everybody.

When we ride the carousel,
we say hello to Canada,
on the other side
of the river.

"Hello, Canada!"

"Hello, Detroit!"

On our last morning, we video chat with Aunt Fancy.

"Aunt Fancy, you said when we complete our Adventure Assignments, we'll discover Detroit. But I'm not sure what that means."

"That's because you haven't seen *The Fist*—a sculpture honoring Joe Louis, the great boxer who never gave up," says Aunt Fancy. "*The Fist* tells the story of Detroit."

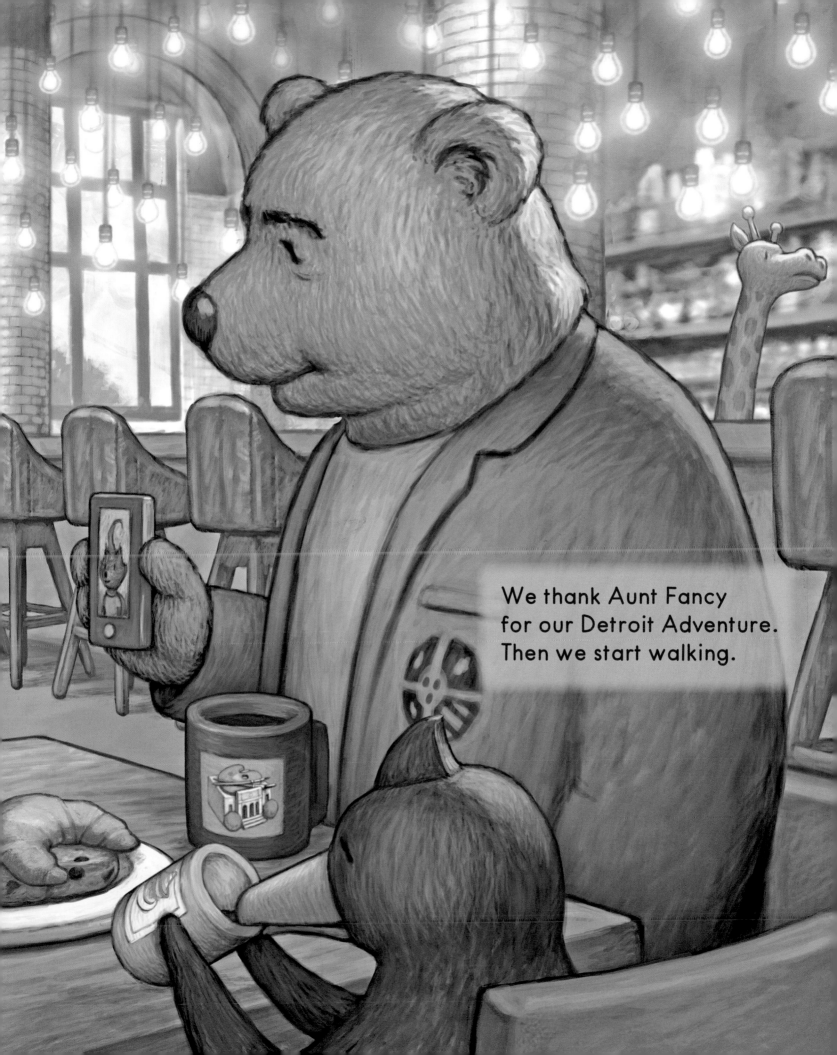

We thank Aunt Fancy
for our Detroit Adventure.
Then we start walking.

And there it is. *The Fist*. Big and strong.

Then it hits me—*POW!*
Detroit is everybody's voice, sounding like one.
It's music and murals and motors . . .

and never giving up.

Now it's time to go home.
We say goodbye to Mr. Reggie.
Lulu says, "Don't forget us, Mr. Reggie."

And he says, "How could I forget you?"
He winks. "You're the cat's pajamas,"
which means he likes us.

Then we wave goodbye to Joe Louis. We wave to Mr. Reggie, Hitsville, coney dogs, roly-poly cherries, and the Tigers. We wave goodbye to Detroit . . .

and Detroit waves back.

MORE TO KNOW!

Detroit is an innovative city bursting with good ideas and people who work together.
Nicknames include: Hitsville U.S.A. (because of the hit songs that came out of Motown),
the Motor City (because Detroit is the heart of the American auto industry), and the
Comeback City (because, like Joe Louis and Henry Ford, Detroit keeps getting better and better).

Belle Isle Park is an island park where you can get out of the city *in the city*. You can fish from a pier, slide down a giant slide, or explore the nature center, conservatory, Dossin Great Lakes Museum, or Belle Isle Aquarium—the oldest aquarium in the country.

Campus Martius Park includes an acre of green space that runs right through the city. "Detroit's Gathering Space" boasts skyline views, gardens, sculptures, a fountain, an ice-skating rink, and an urban beach—400,000 pounds of sand, colorful lounge chairs, and beachside restaurants.

The **Charles H. Wright Museum of African American History** traces the incredible journey of Africans to America—from freedom to bondage to freedom once more—a people who were enslaved but never mastered.

Comerica Park is home to the Detroit Tigers. Besides watching baseball, you can ride a tiger (on a carousel) or a giant baseball (on a Ferris wheel). Nearby is Little Caesars Arena, home of the Red Wings and the Pistons, and Ford Field, home of the Lions.

Coney dogs are a Detroit specialty—a beef hot dog on a steamed bun, topped with special chili sauce, chopped raw onion, and a squiggle of mustard. Next-door neighbors Lafayette and American have battled for coney dog dominance for many years. Who's top dog?

The **Detroit Institute of Arts** has one of the largest art collections in the country. Walk through the gates of Rivera Court to experience the spectacular mural created by Diego Rivera—a tribute to the city's manufacturing base and labor force. Diego Rivera, a famous Mexican muralist, considered this to be his finest work. He believed art belonged on public walls, not in private collections.

The **Detroit International Riverfront** includes 5.5 miles of parks nestled along the Detroit River. The carousel features Detroit fauna, where you can ride a sturgeon or a snail at Cullen Plaza and say hello to Canada right across the river!

Eastern Market is a huge, year-round market committed to a healthy Detroit. It's bursting with fresh produce, meat, cheese, and flowers. And the backdrop for this colorful market? More than 100 murals!

The **Monument to Joe Louis**, also known as **The Fist**, created by sculptor Robert Graham, is a memorial to boxer Joe Louis. Louis, nicknamed the Brown Bomber, is considered one of the greatest heavyweight boxers of all time. He carried a punch inside the ring and out! He fought racial injustice throughout his lifetime.

The **Ford Piquette Avenue Plant** is the birthplace of the first Model T. You can visit Henry Ford's Secret Experimental Room (where only a handful of people were allowed inside!), examine antique cars, and crank the engine with the flywheel magneto.

The **Fox Theatre** is Detroit's crown jewel. Open the golden doors to a gleaming, palacelike performing arts center that boasts some of the top shows in the country.

The **Detroit Foundation Hotel** is a modern hotel, but it used to be the headquarters for the Detroit Fire Department! Big red doors mark the arches where fire trucks once passed, and sleek fire poles commemorate the building's colorful history.

Hitsville U.S.A. is the home of Motown Records, founded by Berry Gordy. The hugely popular Motown Sound is a combination of pop and soul sung by smooth, blended voices. Top artists include the Temptations, Stevie Wonder, the Jackson 5, and Diana Ross and the Supremes.

The **People Mover** is a fully automated, light-rail train that runs on an elevated track through Downtown Detroit. Price: 75 cents.

The next time we're in Detroit, we want to see the amazing Art Deco interior of the Guardian Building, cool off at the water park at Mt. Elliott Plaza, and hit the trail on a snowmobile simulator at the Outdoor Adventure Center.